REMARKABLE PEOPLE

Steve Nash

by Michael De Medeiros

Published by Weigl Publishers Inc.
350 5th Avenue, Suite 3304, PMB 6G
New York, NY 10118-0069

Website: www.weigl.com

Library of Congress Cataloging-in-Publication Data

De Medeiros, Michael
  Steve Nash : remarkable people / Michael De Medeiros.
     p. cm.
  Includes index.
   ISBN 978-1-59036-990-6 (hard cover : alk. paper) -- ISBN 978-1-59036-991-3 (soft
cover : alk. paper)
  1. Nash, Steve, 1974---Juvenile literature. 2. Basketball players--Canada--
Biography--Juvenile literature. I. Title.
   GV884.N37D46 2009
   796.323092--dc22
   [B]

                              2008003967

Printed in the United States of America
1 2 3 4 5 6 7 8 9 0 12 11 10 09 08

Editor: Danielle LeClair
Design: Terry Paulhus

Photograph Credits
Weigl acknowledges Getty Images as the primary image supplier for this title.
Unless otherwise noted, all images herein were obtained from Getty Images and
its contributors.

Other photograph credits include: **Dreamstime**: pages 7 (top right), 13 (bottom);
Corbis: page 12.

Every reasonable effort has been made to trace ownership and to obtain
permission to reprint copyright material. The publishers would be pleased
to have any errors or omissions brought to their attention so that they may
be corrected in subsequent printings.

Contents

Who Is Steve Nash?

Steve Nash is a basketball player. He is one of the best-known players in the National Basketball Association (NBA). In 1996, he started his **professional** basketball career with the Phoenix Suns. Steve is a point guard. A point guard is usually the best ball handler on the team. It is Steve's job to lead the **offense** and pass the ball to his team's top scorers. Steve has won many fans and awards for his skill as a point guard in the NBA. In 2005 and 2006, sports writers across North America voted Steve the Most Valuable Player (MVP) in the league.

"That was the most important thing in my world—playing basketball games."

Growing Up

Stephen John Nash was born on February 7, 1974, in Johannesburg, South Africa. When Steve was 18 months old, his father, John, retired from professional soccer, and the Nash family moved to Regina, Saskatchewan. Saskatchewan is a prairie **province** in Canada. A short while later, Steve and his family moved to Victoria, British Columbia. Victoria is on Vancouver Island, off the west coast of Canada. Steve, his brother Martin, and his sister Joann, all grew up playing soccer. Steve was a talented soccer player. He dreamed of someday playing professionally, like his father.

When Steve was about 12 or 13, a friend asked him to come to the playground to play a game of basketball. Steve fell in love with the game. He tried out for the basketball team at school and was chosen to play. In the eighth grade, during his first season playing basketball, Steve told his mother that he would one day become an NBA star.

■ During his first year of university, Steve bounced a tennis ball everywhere he went to improve his ball-handling skills.

Get to Know Canada

CANADIAN FLAG

NATIONAL ANIMAL

NATIONAL TREE

0   1500 MILES

0   1500 KM

If every Canadian received an equal share of the country, each person would get a piece of land the size of 27 baseball fields.

Canada has the world's longest coastline. It is surrounded by the Pacific Ocean to the west, Atlantic Ocean to the east, and the Arctic Ocean to the north.

Canada has two official languages—French and English.

It was a Canadian, Dr. James Naismith, who invented basketball.

There are nearly 34 million people living in Canada.

Think about it!

Steve lived in Johannesburg, South Africa, for a year and a half before he moved to Canada. Imagine moving to a different country. Make a chart comparing your home to another country. Compare things such as language, weather, food, clothing, jobs, and nature. What would you need to learn about your new home?

Practice Makes Perfect

Steve has been an athlete all his life. When he turned one year old, Steve received a soccer ball for his birthday. As Steve grew, he showed real skill on the **soccer pitch**. He was fast and **agile**. Steve's most important skill was his ability to **analyze** a game. He was able to anticipate what his teammates and his opponents would do. He did well in games that required planning and **strategy**. In elementary school, Steve's ability to use strategy helped him win three chess titles. Steve always knew he wanted to be a professional athlete, but he had trouble deciding what sport to pursue. He played as many sports as he could, including hockey, rugby, soccer, and lacrosse.

■ While in university, Steve was twice named the West Coast Conference Player of the Year.

When Steve started playing basketball, he knew he had found his sport. During school vacations, the years he was in junior high and high school, Steve would spend all day playing basketball. He would often play as many as eight hours a day, long after his friends had gone home for supper.

Steve liked a challenge. He created his own basketball drills and would practice every day. One day, he would complete 500 jump shots before he would let himself go home. Another day, he would have to make 200 free throws. Steve never gave up.

Steve was dedicated to being the best player he could be. His commitment and hard work were inspiring to his teammates. In his last year of high school, Steve led his basketball team to the British Columbia senior boys' AAA championship.

■ Steve is ambidextrous. This means he can use both hands to do things, such as writing, dribbling, and shooting a basketball.

Key Events

Steve's chance to realize his dream of playing in the NBA came in 1992. The head basketball coach from Santa Clara University in California flew to Vancouver to watch Steve play. After the game, Coach Dick Davey offered Steve a full scholarship. The university would pay Steve's **tuition**, housing, and food. Steve just had to do well in his classes and play basketball. Coach Davey told Steve to focus on becoming a complete player. While Steve was a talented point guard, Coach Davey said Steve was the worst **defender** he had ever seen. Steve was willing to do whatever Coach Davey asked of him.

In 1996, Steve's hard work paid off. He graduated from Santa Clara University with a degree in **sociology** and was a **draft pick** for the NBA team, the Phoenix Suns. Steve fulfilled his dream and was a professional basketball player.

In 2001, the Phoenix Suns traded Steve to the Dallas Mavericks. Steve returned to the Phoenix Suns in 2004. The city and his teammates were thrilled.

■ Steve is the first Canadian ever to win NBA MVP.

Thoughts from Steve

Steve has loved sports, especially basketball, since he was a child. Here are a few things he has said about his career and his life.

Steve is proud of his success.

"I would never have dreamed of being MVP first of all, let alone twice."

Being the best player he can be is important to Steve.

"There are a lot of great players in this league, but to be put in the upper group was something I always expected of myself."

Some people worried Steve would never play professional basketball.

"You know, I never really lost the belief that something would arise. I just thought: 'Hang in there and you'll get an opportunity.' And I did."

Steve is a determined athlete.

"You've just got to do the things you've always done and don't let your life hinge on shots going in or out."

Steve remembers where he came from.

"It seems like my whole life I've been this little Canadian kid dreaming somebody would give me a chance."

Steve is a team player.

"I love being part of a team, any team. Not just playing, but the **camaraderie**, the whole thing."

What Is a Basketball Player?

Basketball is a team sport. It was invented in 1891 as an energetic game that could be played indoors during the winter. It combined rules from football, soccer, and hockey. The game quickly became popular. In 1898, the first professional basketball league was formed.

When playing a competitive game of basketball, there are hoops, called baskets, on either end of the court. Each team has five players. The teams get points by putting the ball in the other team's basket. The team that scores the most points wins the game.

Each player on a basketball team has a specific role. Some protect their team from being scored on. Others score baskets, or points. Professional basketball players are athletes. They train very hard to be good at their sport.

Most professional basketball players are tall. The average height of a player in the NBA is 6 feet 7 inches (2.04 meters) tall. Steve is one of the shortest players on his team. He is 6 feet 3 inches (1.9 m) tall.

■ When basketball was first invented, the hoops were peach baskets. Each time someone scored, the referee would climb on a ladder to get the ball out of the basket.

Basketball Players 101

Wilt Chamberlain (1936–1999)

Team: Los Angeles Lakers, Philadelphia 76ers, and San Francisco Warriors

Achievements: At 7 feet 1 inch (2.2 m) tall, Wilt Chamberlain was an impressive and talented basketball player. Wilt dominated basketball. Opposing teams would try almost anything to stop him from scoring. Wilt was a four-time NBA MVP and two-time winner of the NBA Championships. Wilt was named to the NBA All-Star team seven times. He became known as "Wilt the Stilt" and "The Big Dipper."

Kareem Abdul-Jabbar (1947–)

Team: Los Angeles Lakers and Milwaukee Bucks

Achievements: Kareem Abdul-Jabbar is one of the most recognizable players in the history of basketball. He retired from professional basketball in 1989, at 42 years old. At that time, no other player had played as many seasons, scored as many points, won as many MVP awards, played in as many All-Star games, or blocked more shots.

Michael Jordan (1963–)

Team: Chicago Bulls and Washington Wizards

Achievements: Micheal Jordan is one of the most popular professional athletes in recent history. Michael's abilities and commitment to basketball helped him and his teammates excel at the game. He was a five-time NBA MVP, played in 14 All-Star games, and helped his teams win six championships. Michael was skilled at every part of the game. He became known as "Air Jordan."

Shaquille O'Neal (1972–)

Team: Los Angeles Lakers, Orlando Magic, Miami Heat, and Phoenix Suns

Achievements: Standing 7 feet 1 inch (2.2 m) tall, Shaquille O'Neal is one of the most talented players in the sport. Other teams often put two defensive players against him to keep him from scoring. He is a two-time NBA MVP. Shaq is strong and powerful. Once, during a college basketball game, he **dunked** the ball and tore the basket completely off the backboard.

Basketballs

Most basketballs have an inflatable bladder, which is a rubber, ball-like container. The bladder is filled with air and wrapped in layers of fiber. It is then covered with a bumpy surface, which is usually made from real or **synthetic** leather. A standard basketball is 29.5 inches (74.9 centimeters) and has about 4,118 pebbles, or bumps. The NBA ball is orange with black divider marks, or ribs.

Influences

Steve has had two main influences in his life. The first and most important is his family. Steve's parents encouraged hard work and dedication to school and sports. His father, John, and his mother, Jean, believed that children should be encouraged to play sports. It taught them important values, such as **vision**, commitment, and drive. Steve's brother, Martin, plays professional soccer for the Vancouver Whitecaps. Steve's sister, Joann, was captain of the University of Victoria soccer team for three years.

Other major influences in Steve's life are his coaches. In high school, Coach Ian Hyde-Lay believed Steve was good enough to play college basketball. He wrote letters and sent videotapes of Steve to more than 30 universities and colleges in the United States. Ian did not give up on Steve or his dream.

■ In 2005, Steve's coach on the Phoenix Suns, Mike D'Antoni, was named NBA coach of the year, just two days after Steve won the NBA's Most Valuable Player.

Dick Davey recognized Steve's potential and coached him to be a successful all-around player. Steve believes that he is successful because of his coaches. He says that they were hard on him and pushed him to develop as a player. Steve thinks that he would never have had a chance to play in the NBA without his coaches.

THE NASH FAMILY

Steve is very close to his family. Though he left Canada to play basketball, Steve spends as much time as he can with them. Steve believes his brother Martin is the best athlete in the family, and he admires his sister and her athletic skills. During the winter, Steve's parents live in Phoenix to be near Steve, his wife Alejandra, and their twin daughters, Lola and Bella. Steve's mother, Jean, has said that she is very proud of Steve for working so hard and achieving his dream of playing professional basketball. She is most proud of the good person he has become.

■ Steve's wife, Alejandra, was born and raised in Paraguay. Steve donates time and money to charities in Paraguay to support his wife and her heritage.

Overcoming Obstacles

When Steve was drafted by the Phoenix Suns in 1996, he was the 15th round pick. This means that Steve was overlooked by NBA teams 14 times before he was chosen. NBA scouts were concerned that Steve was too small to play in the NBA. When the Phoenix Suns announced that Steve was one of their draft picks, the fans booed. They were angry and disappointed that the Suns had drafted Steve.

At first, the Phoenix Suns did not give Steve much court time. In 1998, Steve was traded. That year, there was a conflict between the NBA players and the team owners. It was a short season and a hard year for Steve.

■ Steve wears number 13. He chose number 13 because, when he joined the Phoenix Suns, his college number, 11, was taken.

Steve was playing poorly, and every time he got on the floor, the fans would boo him. Steve did not complain or make excuses, even though he was suffering with injuries. He had a painful injury in his right foot and developed a back problem.

Steve suffers from a medical condition that causes problems in people's backs. One of the **vertebrae** in the spine moves forward. This makes the muscles around the area tight. For Steve, it is very difficult to play when he has back pain. One of the ways he protects his back is to lie flat on the floor during timeouts or when he is not playing. Sitting on the bench compresses his vertebrae together and makes the pain in his back worse.

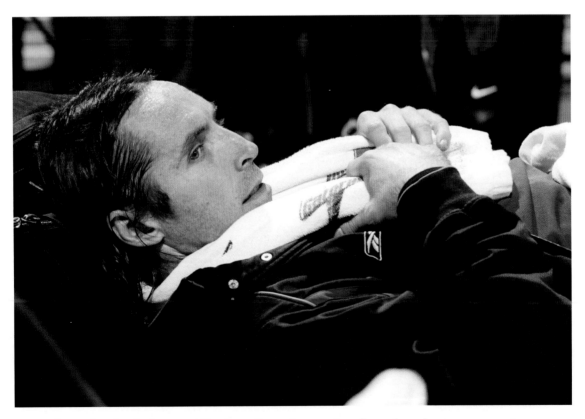

■ To keep his back from stiffening, Steve has to lay flat when he is not moving. When he is standing, Steve has to keep moving. His assistant coach says Steve wiggles and twitches so much he looks like he has ants in his pants.

Achievements and Successes

Steve has won many awards and honors. During his first year of high school, Steve was named British Columbia's most valuable player in soccer. In the year 2000, Steve was captain of the Canadian Olympic basketball team. It was the first time the Canadian basketball team had qualified for the Olympics in 12 years.

In his professional career, Steve has won many awards. He won the league MVP two years in a row, played on the NBA All-Star team five times, and for three years, Steve led the league in assists per game. In 2006, he had the highest **free-throw** percentage in the NBA, with 0.921. This means that when Steve gets a free throw, he scores 92 percent of the time.

■ Before going to the 2000 Olympics as captain of the Canadian team, Steve gave the Canadian coach $25,000. He told his coach to give each player on the team money to cover travel expenses.

All of these accomplishments make it possible for Steve to help others around the world. In 2001, he formed the Steve Nash Foundation. The foundation helps disadvantaged children. It fights **poverty**, abuse, neglect, and illness. Steve recently used the money he earned **endorsing** a product to pay for a new children's ward in a hospital in Paraguay. Another charity Steve supports is the GuluWalk organization. With his help, this group raises money and awareness for children affected by war in Uganda. Steve loves helping people, and he cares about the world around him.

Steve runs the Steve Nash Youth Basketball League in British Columbia, Canada. This basketball program helps kids from ages of five to 13 develop basketball skills. Steve started the youth basketball league to get kids interested and excited about physical activity and sports.

MOST INFLUENTIAL PEOPLE

In May 2006, Steve was named one of *Time* magazine's 100 most **influential** people in the world. The article about Steve was written by former NBA legend Charles Barkley. Charles said that Steve is a person who works incredibly hard. He wrote that Steve is a hero and a nice person. Charles said that people look up to Steve for his commitment to being a great player and human being. To find out more the *Time* top 100 most influential people, visit **www.time.com/time/specials/2007/time100**.

Write a Biography

A person's life story can be the subject of a book. This kind of book is called a biography. Biographies describe the lives of remarkable people, such as those who have achieved great success or have done important things to help others. These people may be alive today, or they may have lived many years ago. Reading a biography can help you learn more about a remarkable person.

At school, you might be asked to write a biography. First, decide who you want to write about. You can choose an athlete, such as Steve Nash, or any other person you find interesting. Then, find out if your library has any books about this person. Learn as much as you can about him or her. Write down the key events in this person's life. What was this person's childhood like? What has he or she accomplished? What are his or her goals? What makes this person special or unusual?

A concept web is a useful research tool. Read the questions in the following concept web. Answer the questions in your notebook. Your answers will help you write your biography review.

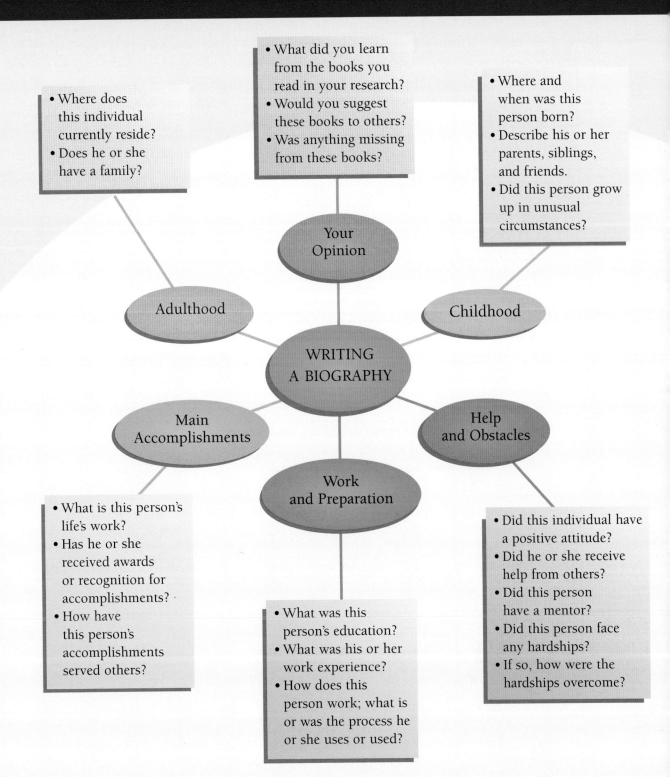

- Where does this individual currently reside?
- Does he or she have a family?

- What did you learn from the books you read in your research?
- Would you suggest these books to others?
- Was anything missing from these books?

- Where and when was this person born?
- Describe his or her parents, siblings, and friends.
- Did this person grow up in unusual circumstances?

Your Opinion

Adulthood

Childhood

WRITING A BIOGRAPHY

Main Accomplishments

Help and Obstacles

Work and Preparation

- What is this person's life's work?
- Has he or she received awards or recognition for accomplishments?
- How have this person's accomplishments served others?

- What was this person's education?
- What was his or her work experience?
- How does this person work; what is or was the process he or she uses or used?

- Did this individual have a positive attitude?
- Did he or she receive help from others?
- Did this person have a mentor?
- Did this person face any hardships?
- If so, how were the hardships overcome?

Timeline

YEAR	STEVE NASH	WORLD EVENTS
1974	Steve is born in Johannesburg, South Africa, on February 7.	The Philadelphia Flyers become the first expansion team in the National Hockey League (NHL) to win the Stanley Cup.
1992	Steve graduates from St. Michael's University School.	On April 1, the NHL has its first strike.
1993	Steve is given a full basketball scholarship to Santa Clara University.	Michael Jordan leads the Chicago Bulls to their third straight NBA championship.
1995	Steve is drafted into the NBA by the Phoenix Suns.	Mickey Mantle, Baseball Hall of Fame center fielder, dies on August 13.
2005	Steve is named the NBA's Most Valuable Player.	The Chicago White Sox win the World Series for the first time since 1917.
2005	Steve is named the NBA's Most Valuable Player for the second year in a row.	The NHL's Carolina Hurricanes win the Stanley Cup.
2008	With Nike, Steve develops a basketball shoe called *Nike Trash Talk*. The shoe is made from 100 percent recycled materials.	Shaquille O'Neal is traded to the Phoenix Suns. Shaq and Steve play on a team together for the first time.

Further Research

How can I find out more about Steve Nash?

Most libraries have computers that connect to a database that contains information on books and articles about different subjects. You can input a key word and find material on that person, place, or thing you want to learn more about. The computer will provide you with a list of books in the library that contain information on the subject you searched for. Non-fiction books are arranged numerically, using their call number. Fiction books are organized alphabetically by the author's last name.

Websites

To learn more about Steve Nash, visit
www.nba.com/playerfile/steve_nash

Learn about basketball at
www.nba.com

Get to know more about
Steve's foundation at
www.stevenash.org

Words to Know

agile: able to move quickly and easily

analyze: closely examine and explain

camaraderie: friendship, good humor, and closeness among a group

defender: a player who tries to prevent the other team from scoring

draft pick: a person chosen to join a team in a professional league

dunked: to slam a basketball through the basket from above

endorsing: to provide support for a product through an advertising campaign

free-throw: a shot at the basket from the foul line, sometimes called a foul shot

influential: someone who has a great impact on others or events

offense: the players on a team who try to score

poverty: people living in circumstances where there is not enough food, money, or opportunity to support themselves

professional: a person who earns money by doing an activity

province: a part of a country, similar to a state

scout: people who look for new sports or entertainment talent

soccer pitch: the field on which a soccer game is played

sociology: the study of the people, groups, institutions, and relationships that make up human society

strategy: a plan to achieve a particular goal

synthetic: a human-made product

tuition: the money a student pays for being taught at a college or university

vertebrae: one of the sections of bone or cartilage that make up the spinal column

vision: the ability to look toward the future

Index